It's the Law!

Carlos Hernandez

INFOMAX
Common Core
READERS

Rosen Classroom™

New York

Published in 2013 by The Rosen Publishing Group, Inc.
29 East 21st Street, New York, NY 10010

Copyright © 2013 by The Rosen Publishing Group, Inc.

All rights reserved. No part of this book may be reproduced in any form without permission in writing from the publisher, except by a reviewer.

Book Design: Michael Harmon

Photo Credits: Cover JustASC/Shutterstock.com; p. 4 Comstock Images/Thinkstock.com; p. 5 Creatas/Thinkstock.com; pp. 6, 7, 10, 21, 22 iStockphoto/Thinkstock.com; p. 8 Onur ERSIN/Shutterstock.com; p. 9 Joe Gough/Shutterstock.com; p. 11 Robert Shafer/Brand X Pictures/Getty Images; p. 12 Ryan McVay/Photodisc/Getty Images; p. 13 trekandshoot/Shutterstock.com; p. 14 Kate Connes/Shutterstock.com; p. 16 michaeljung/Shutterstock.com; p. 17 Lori Martin/Shutterstock.com; p. 18 Lisa F. Young/Shutterstock.com; p. 19 sonya etchinson/Shutterstock.com; p. 20 Darrin Klimek/Digital Vision/Getty Images.

ISBN: 978-1-4488-9073-6
6-pack ISBN: 978-1-4488-9074-3

Manufactured in the United States of America

CPSIA Compliance Information: Batch #WS12RC: For further information contact Rosen Publishing, New York, New York at 1-800-237-9932.

Word Count: 475

Contents

Following the Rules	4
Laws	6
Making Laws	12
How Laws Are Made	15
Our Laws	16
Glossary	23
Index	24

Following the Rules

When you're at home, you might have to follow some rules. Your parents might tell you when to go to bed, or they may give you jobs to do.

Your teacher gives you rules, too. You have to raise your hand before you talk. You also have to ask to leave the classroom. These rules keep everything fair.

Laws

Every home and school has different rules. However, there are some rules that everyone in the United States must follow. These rules are called laws.

A law is a rule that our **government** makes. Laws are like rules, but they're more important. You can get in trouble if you break a law.

Every country makes its own laws, so laws are different around the world. Countries have laws so they can keep people safe and happy.

In the United States, we have laws that tell us what we can and can't do. Do you know what kinds of laws we have?

We have different kinds of laws in the United States.

There are state laws and **national** laws.

Everyone in the country must follow national laws.

States get to make their own laws. These laws work only in that state, but every state has to follow national laws.

Making Laws

Do you know how laws are made? They start off as a bill. A bill explains why something should become a law. A government leader has to write the bill.

Next, other leaders have to read the bill. If they like it, they **vote** to make it a law. More than half of the leaders in **Congress** have to vote for the bill.

Then, the president gets the bill. If he likes it, he signs it and makes it a law. Only the most important bills become laws.

How Laws Are Made

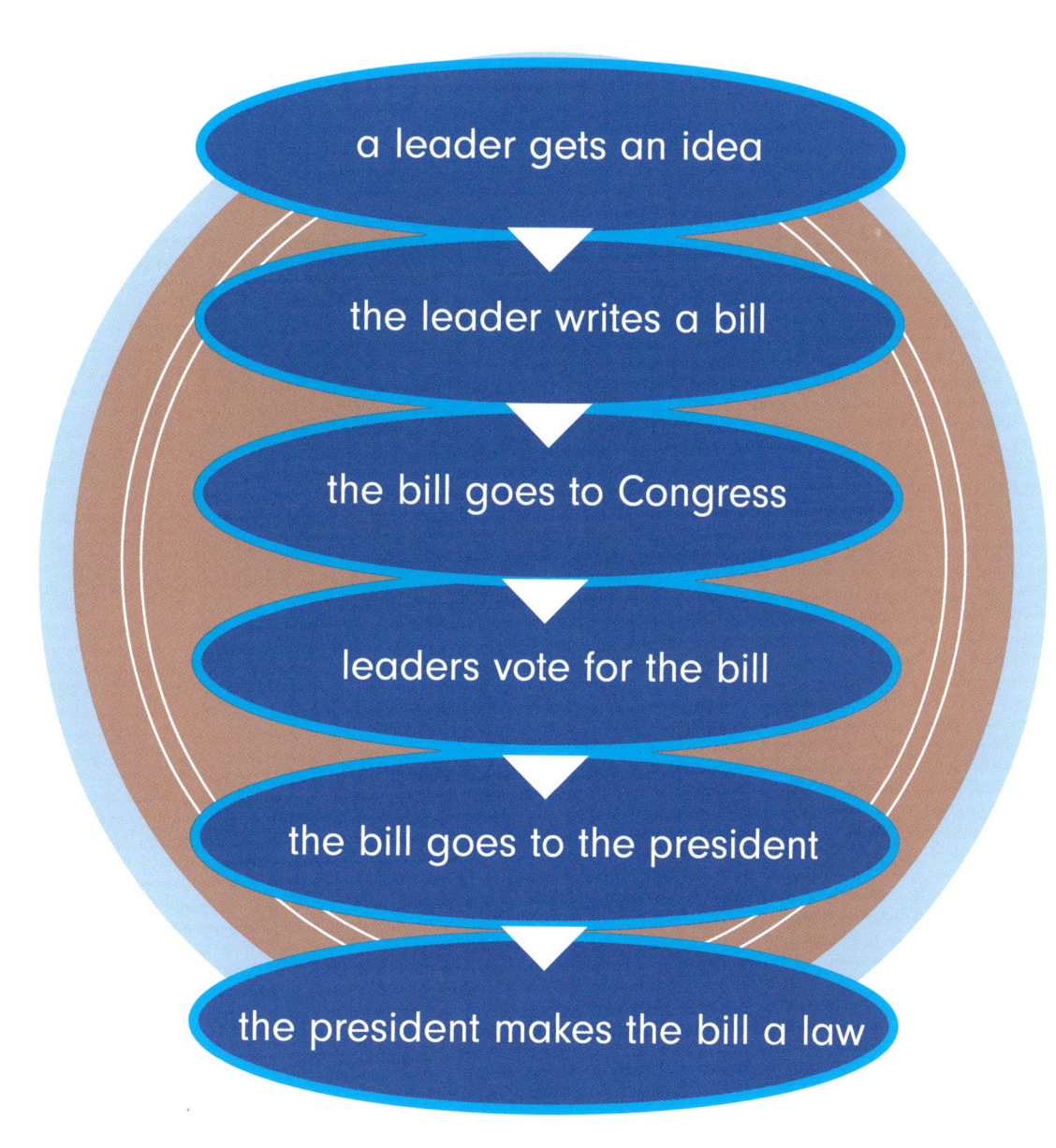

- a leader gets an idea
- the leader writes a bill
- the bill goes to Congress
- leaders vote for the bill
- the bill goes to the president
- the president makes the bill a law

Our Laws

Laws are important because they **protect** the rights that all Americans have. These rights help make the United States a great place to live.

One law gives us the right to say what we want. Long ago, people got in trouble if they said something others didn't like. Today, the law protects our right to say our **opinion**.

There are many other laws, too. One law is that you have to take a test before you can drive a car. This makes sure that everyone knows how to drive safely.

Another law is that we have to wear seatbelts when we're in a car. This makes sure that we don't get hurt. It's important to follow this law.

Some people make sure that everyone follows the laws. They're called police officers. They have a very important job.

Police officers work in our towns and cities to keep us safe. They catch people who break the law. Police officers are very brave.

It's important for all people to follow the laws.

Laws keep us safe and help us do the right thing!

Glossary

Congress (KAHN-gruhs) One part of the United States government.

government (GUH-vurhn-muhnt) A group of people who rule a country, state, or city.

national (NAH-shuh-nuhl) Something having to do with the entire country.

opinion (uh-PIHN-yuhn) How you feel about something.

protect (pruh-TEHKT) To keep something safe.

vote (VOHT) To pick something.

Index

bill(s), 12, 13, 14, 15

Congress, 13, 15

country(ies), 8, 10

fair, 5

government, 7, 12

leader(s), 12, 13, 15

national laws, 10, 11

police officers, 20, 21

president, 14, 15

right(s), 16, 17

safe(ly), 8, 19, 22

state laws, 10, 11

United States, 6, 9, 10, 16

vote, 13, 15